Ways of Seeing

Rick Vick

Chapeltown Books

British Library Cataloguing in Publication Data

A Record of this Publication is available from the British Library

ISBN 978-1-910542-65-1

This edition published 2021 by Chapeltown Books
Manchester, England

Contents

Introduction

I first met Rick Vick around the millennium in the local college of further education, at my first ever attendance at a poetry evening class. He sat top table, gaunt faced, nicotine toothed, spike-stubbled, undulating grey hair down to his bony shoulders, spectacles on the end of his hairy nose, crooked as his infectious smile.

By his side lay a leather satchel, which I later learnt contained a copy of the Greek myths, Shakespeare's sonnets and a selection of the cheapest books of poetry he could find that particular week from the high street charity shop. And notebooks, lots of notebooks. He welcomed the shy table of the middle-class, middle aged, with his cut-glass accent - enunciated vowels, clipped consonants and the seldom heard use of the personal pronoun 'One' rather than I or You. Once a week, from our clunky, wooden beginnings, Rick coaxed out lines from our generally dysfunctional existences that had us weeping in front of strangers and hugging them at home time.

His mantra was, 'Let the pen do the writing.'

Rick was from select British bloodstock - private boarding school from a young age, his father a high-court judge and his grandfather, a Lord Mayor of London. He started his writing career as a journalist on London's Fleet Street but quickly discovered the hack's life wasn't for him and, with a dinner jacket in a suitcase, travelled to New York, where he met a girl and her cat and drove to the hippy communes of California.

From that moment on, Rick never had a penny to spare, but he travelled the world and wrote and lived with authors, poets and artists. He spent fourteen years on the Greek island of Hydra during the 1960s where he led the Bohemian lifestyle with the likes of Leonard Cohen, Cohen's lover Marianne Jensen, and where Lawrence Durrell, Henry Miller, Cyril Connolly and Patrick Leigh Fermor were literary visitors.

A decade after the evening classes, I met Rick leading The Ale House Poets group in Stroud, Gloucestershire where he'd settled with his family. He charged £5 a person for three hours of creative writing exercises, readings and conversation. The group members were seldom able to lay their hands on a £5 note, so he'd settle for a half pint of beer or a cigarette. Without any doubt, Rick kindled in me, and many others, a passion for words and writing that has continued to this day. But more than writing, Rick had a deep love of all art forms, of being true to one's inner calling, and of humanity in all its guises.

In Stroud, Rick was a busy and interested activist rather than a local politician. He had a genuine love for the town and its cultural life. For many years he helped organise the Stroud Arts Festival including poetry, dance, theatre, music and painting. He had a love of people that manifested itself on every level, from the encouragement of a shy, new poet at one of his workshops to his record-breaking seven appearances as a writer at the prestigious Stroud Short Stories.

Rick saw no difference between, and spoke no differently to, the homeless person sleeping rough in the doorway or the well-to-do visitor to the art gallery or poetry reading holding a complimentary glass of wine. During his life in Stroud, he was involved in social work, leading creative writing classes for ex-offenders and those with addiction issues.

The last time I saw Rick he was terminally ill in bed. He told me of the books he was reading and of how much he'd enjoyed reading a modest piece of my work he'd seen recently in an online journal. I told him that my writing life was entirely thanks to his teaching.

'Nonsense,' he said. 'I was simply the facilitator. Let the pen do the writing.'

Steven John
The Phare Magazine - Joint Founder and Managing Editor

Seeing

He watches her, at first vaguely – an old woman paddling. So he sees her through his seven-year-old eyes – although she is no more than forty, a few years older than his mother. She is standing in the tattered lace of the wave's furthest reach up the beach. She is alone. Not just by herself, he thinks, having some notion of what alone means, being an only child. Something about her stillness keeps his eyes fixed on her. She is not like the mothers and a few fathers further up the beach, beyond the breakwater, ankle deep in the cold North Sea, keeping eyes on their children, further out, splashing and screaming with abandon.

As he watches he senses a tremor in her body as she lifts her head and stares out to sea. He follows her gaze to the distant smudge of the horizon. There is not much to see: no boats just the undulations of the waves. She is wearing a dark red dress which, unlike the other women in the shallows, she has not gathered in her hand to lift.

She steps forward and keeps on moving, slowly, into the incoming waves. He glances towards his mother, who is unpacking triangles of sandwiches and three bananas from two plastic boxes, laying them on a small square of white cloth. He is about to call her attention to the woman but seeing the tight line of her mouth decides against disturbing her. His father had said he would not come on the picnic outing as he had a fiver on the 4.15 at Doncaster. She had not been pleased.

She is up to her thighs when he looks back. Something in him knows what she is doing but he has not the language to put his intuition into words. Deeper and deeper she goes, the sea up almost to her waist. The dress has risen up around her. Like a dingy come to rescue her, he thinks.

She lifts her hand to her head and frees a clasp or pin that holds the long dark hair that falls to her shoulders.

On and on she pushes. He feels her effort. She stops. The ocean heaves all around her body up to her chest. He looks up the beach. No one has seen her. He wants to shout out, to point but does not.

Quite suddenly she raises her arms fingers outstretched and dips under the water and is gone. Just like that. He hugs his knees hard in his arms, staring. Staring so hard – willing her to reappear. She does not.

No one else has noticed. He looks around. All is just as it was the last time he had looked and he wonders if he had seen, truly seen, what he had seen.

Flight

In the end there wasn't an ending, at least not the one she was expecting. When she jumped there was no doubt in her mind as her body obeyed the last impulse. Gravity, finally her ally, as she plummeted through the freedom of space.

That she landed on a barge loaded with cotton waste was the greatest surprise of her life. No one had seen her jump and the skipper had not noticed her arrival on his cargo. She had lain there in the dark, puzzled and wondering if this was how death felt, cocooned. She was aggravated to be still thinking. Then about the time the thumping engine became silent at the dock she noticed that she was no longer at odds with herself. She felt a feather light ease as she hopped over the side and slipped from the harbour and padded forth to meet her new life, only mildly regretful of having taken off her shoes before she climbed the railing of the golden bridge.

Mazurka

Her mother stood alert outside the circle of boys and girls sitting on the carpet as her daughter, Faye, un-wrapped her birthday presents. She had cautioned her tomboy to say 'thank you' even if she did not like the gift. She knew well the Polish fire that simmered in the just turned seven year old. 'You don't want to hurt feelings, do you?' Faye had shrugged.

She did not much like the woolly hat knowing she would not wear it even though she liked blue, the colour of her eyes. The colouring book she might have appreciated a year or two ago and the crayons she saw at once were cheap, not near as good as the ones she already had. The black Stetson she immediately put on smiling at the boy whose gift it was. When she ripped off the pink paper around a box that revealed a pouting long legged Barbie doll, her mother saw her intent and before Faye could hurl it away, she reached out and held onto the box meeting her daughter's furious eyes. She raised her brows a fraction. Faye stamped her western boots then forced a whispered, 'Thank you.'

When the last of her friends had gone she sat on the carpet staring at the strewn paper and presents. She picked up the woolly hat, sniffed it and was about to put it on then tossed it aside. Her mother was in the kitchen washing up. She glanced at a card leaning against a lamp on a side table. Behind the hand-drawn dancing figure on the outside, she could just see the corners of bank notes clipped to the inside. She angrily wiped a tear from her face. She

13

had felt happy before the party but now she felt sad. Not sad that it was over. No, her sadness was bigger than that. It was an emptiness she felt; a feeling she had often when she thought of her father, gone nearly a year now to another lady. She was angry too. Her fists were clenched. The feeling was like the pecking of a small bird deep in her belly.

She heard the flap of the letter box. There on the door mat was a bundle of newspaper tied haphazardly round and round with string. She bent and picked it up – it was as light as nothing. She raised it to her face, sniffed and wrinkled her nose. It smelt mouldy.

She tore off the string and damp newspaper to reveal an old rope knotted at each end. A picture formed in her mind. A grizzled white bearded man sitting in the doorway of the now boarded up sweet and tobacco shop on the corner where she caught the school bus. She could picture the rope tied around the old dirty coat he wore. She had remembered how her father put coins in the up-turned hats of street sleepers so she had, almost every morning, put a few pennies of her lunch money in the old man's hat. Sometimes he played a violin still sitting. His trousers were pinned up below the knees of both legs and there were a pair of wooden crutches leant against the wall. She liked listening to the tunes he played, though sometimes they made her feel sad. He smiled up at her when she dropped the coins into the hat. How did he know, she thought, and where I live? Had he overheard talk about her party by the children at the bus stop? She heard her father's voice, 'When in doubt create a mystery.'

14

She clenched a knot in each hand and swung the rope back and forth in front of her legs then began to skip. Slowly at first jumping high then faster and faster she swung the rope till her feet were a blur. On and on and on she swung and jumped, her boots thudding on the wooden floor. Her mother came out of the kitchen, smiled to see her daughter in flight.

The next day Faye took one of the bank notes from the card and folded it as tight as she could. Just before she hopped onto the school bus she turned and tossed it into the old man's hat. He looked up and smiled and raising his bow played the opening chords of a wild Polish Mazurka folk dance as the bus pulled away.

Cranes

'Nine hundred and eighty,' she whispers tossing the intricately folded paper crane into the wicker basket beside her on the floor. She flexes her fingers, takes a swig from the bottle of Scotch on the low table before her, and reaches to the piled sheets of rice paper. Her reflection in the glass doors grows stronger as the dusk thickens.

She folds quickly, hardly looking at her fingers. She tilts back on her crossed legs and looks up through the skylight to the first stars. Her hands continue to move, folding, smoothing, tucking until another is formed. She holds it to the light of oil lamp, turns it about, frowns and tosses it into the open door of the wood stove where it flares briefly.

'One thousand.' She tosses the bird into the air, catches it and drops it into the basket. 'Now.' She lights a cigarette, inhales deeply and putting the full basket on the low table, bends and plunges in her hands, moves them about sensually then stands, takes the basket in her arms and walks to the doors.

The lake stretches still and dark from the narrow beach. She steps in, and squats with the basket at arm's reach by her side. She picks out a crane and, with a lighter, sets flame to the tail and drops it on the water where it bobs scattering shadows. A breeze catches at it, turns it about, pushes it out over the dark sheen.

She takes another and another in quick succession setting fire to each and dropping it into the water until the lake is a dance of fire. The last one she holds close to her chest, bends her head and whispers before lighting and setting it adrift.

She stands and stares for a few moments then unties her kimono and shrugs it off. Her arms raised above her head, she dives, surfacing a few yards out, her black hair a dark corona about her head. She swims with a powerful stroke creating wavelets that sets the burning birds bobbing. At the still centre of the lake, surrounded by dancing flames, she rolls onto her back and shouts, 'Echo.'

'Echo' reverberates back from the darkly wooded shore.

She floats awhile, arms outstretched, her hair streaming out around her then, as the last flames dies, she lifts her arms skywards and submerges.

Ways of Seeing

'How come their God's different from ours, Miss?' a young girl twirling her hair between her fingers asked.

'Yeah, and how come they say there is only one God that's their God?' a boy, about eight, added.

'And what about our God, Miss? We know Him, don't we and what He looks like, don't we?' a girl at the back of the class called out.

Miss smiled. 'Do we?'

'Course we do,' the first girl cried out. 'I see Him often. My Gran's got a picture of Him on the wall over her bed.'

'I've seen Him too up there in the clouds, long white beard an' all,' another boy said. Some of the children looked at him and there were a few nudges and titters.

'That's right, an' He's on the roof of that church somewhere. Italy or Spain, somewhere like that.'

'The Sistine Chapel in Rome. That's where the picture is, on the ceiling,' Miss replied.

'What about their God then? What's He look like?' the first girl asked, a little aggressively. I never seen pictures of Him. Not one.'

'Nor me. I bet they don't have any, do they,' the first boy said.

'No, they don't, you're right. But that doesn't mean He doesn't exist for them. They believe in God just like some of us do. He's everywhere. They say, He can't be put in a picture, that's all.'

The children looked puzzled. The teacher was silent a moment. She looked around the classroom at the eager young faces looking up at her. There were twenty-six eight- and nine-year-olds.

'Here's what we will do. Let's all go to the windows and look out and see what's out there.' There was a scraping of chairs, a chattering of young voices and they all, girls and boys, stood at the two tall windows looking out at the playground, the trees beyond and the cloud jostled, lowering sky above. For two or three minutes they stood there almost silent, almost still.

'Ok. Now I'd like you to go back to your desks and write down what you saw. Everything you saw.'

Back at their desks the children wrote and wrote, almost silently, for five minutes or so. Miss Gyles stood looking out of the window until she heard the pencils cease their scratching.

'Now, who wants to read out what they've written?' Five hands shot up. Three girls and two boys read. Each was different. Different descriptions of the trees, sky, playground.

'Good,' she said. 'Now let's go back to the window and look again but this time I want you to see what you did not see last time, maybe things you can't see, like what there might be under the bark of the trees, behind the trees, in the grass and in the earth, and what didn't you see in the sky, in the clouds and far, far away.'

The children giggled. Some looked bewildered. Back at the window they were silent, staring, and when they returned to their desks and started writing their pencils scratched for minutes and minutes, much longer than before.

Miss Gyles was at her desk, writing also.

Making a Baby

I remember the day me and my sis decided to make a baby, even the time cos she had just thrown the old tin alarm clock that sat on top of the fridge at me – it was 3.32. The hands are stuck at that now, six months on. At least I think it's six months, 'cos it was snowing then and it's hot and sticky now.

It was snowing 'cos we asked Santa for snow so it must have been Christmas. Yes, it was Christmas. That was why she threw the clock at me. Mum – we didn't call her Mum but she was, we was sure; Sis looks just like her, lots of rusty hair and a pinched sorta nose – had gone out before what was supposed to be our Christmas dinner. And Dad, who was never at home anyways, had not brought any food for us an' we was hungry, pissed off and only had one present between us – a wind-up train and I, the boy, thought I should have it. After she threw the clock and missed me we was bored and looking for something to do. We poked about in Dad's shed down the garden where he kept some old tools, mostly rusted, and empty tins of baccy. We found some magazines there of naked men and women doing stuff with each other.

'That's how they make babies,' Dora said.

She was a bit older than me. Looked complicated. More like wrestling.

'Are you sure?' I asked.

'Course, silly,' she said. 'It's obvious, look.'

I couldn't see anything obvious at all.

'Then why women doing stuff with other women?' I asked her.

Dora frowned. 'Could be how girl babies are made,' she said.

That's when she asked me if I wanted to try it out – making babies that is. 'We just do what they're doing in the pictures,' she said. 'Simple.'

'Then what?' I said. 'You'd have a baby. What would you do with it?'

'Look at us. They don't know what to do with us. We must've started the same way.' She scrunched her nose. 'Something to do, innit? Telly's broke and oh, I don't know, I'd quite like a little thing like a baby around. Better'n you, anyways.'

'What do we do first then?' I asked feeling kinda tingly. Blimey, I was only seven 'What would we do with a baby?'

'Gotta get undressed, get naked like them, I suppose,' she said. 'Look at the pictures.'

I looked and suddenly didn't much like what I saw. I felt very small and a bit sad. Dora looked at me kinda funny. I knew that look, her eyes big as marbles and bright like she was seeing inside of me.

'Never mind,' she said. 'Let's go down the park instead. Maybe I'll save up and get a rabbit or something.'

As Easy as That

A seat in the shadows, almost invisible. That is what I like, to imagine I'm mostly unseen, though of course, I'm not to those who spot the old fellow in the corner. Invisibility is a trick; one learned, I am told by secret agents. The first lesson is that you have to not want to be seen. The second is to never ever return even a glance to a noticing eye. Only Joe, the barman, knows who I am, where I am and keeps me supplied with Jack Daniels discreetly delivered to my small corner table tucked away at the back of the room. I'm here almost every day and often into the evening. It is where I do much of my writing.

There is only one other person in the bar. A young woman at the far end of the long curved black marble counter, near where Joe sits with his racing paper when there's no one about and he can watch the door. She came in soon after I. She has been sipping her martini for a while now, sitting there silently on a tall stool. Is she waiting for someone I wonder? She is young, mid-twenties, long dark hair, and has the air of someone new to New York. I'm not sure why I think that. Perhaps it is the way she's sat there casually, like a younger girl swinging her legs now and then. I guess she's from Ohio or maybe Canada, even. Canadians often do have a surprising innocence. She is not a street-girl, of that I am sure.

He pushes the swing doors open with a black leather gloved hand. There is a sprinkling of snow on the shoulders of his dark overcoat that vanishes in the warmth of the room. He is purposeful; a hint of a swagger in his walk to the bar. The homburg hat, tilted at a slight angle, shadows his youngish face, thirtyish – maybe younger. He hoiks a stool towards him with his foot and unbuttoning his coat sits. He takes off the hat. His features, un-shadowed are strong. His nose, almost too large, runs in a straight line from his thick dark brows. Italian origin I guess, Napoli or maybe further south. I hope not Sicily. He has still not noticed the woman at the end of the bar. Joe continues reading his newspaper, he misses nothing.

The man has taken off his gloves, puts them one on top of the other to his left and places his hands palm downwards on the counter. Almost imperceptibly he lets his taut spring unwind. His shoulders drop a little. He moistens his lips with the tip of his tongue and looks down at his hands, focussing on the large gold ring on the index finger of his left hand. Relaxed he has shed some years. He now looks boyish and even reveals a hint of uncertainty.

She's watching him too, twirling the swizzle stick in the cocktail glass in front of her. I *wonder* if she's seen his mask slip, his vulnerability glimmer through. She must have for she slips from her stool, walks along the full length of the bar and touches him on the shoulder. He swivels towards her and looks up. This is one of the few cities in the world that allows, even encourages women to approach men.

'Hi,' she says. One glance into her wide eyes, brown I guess, and open smile tells him she is not on the make.

'Hi,' he replies. There is a moment's hesitancy.

24

She sits on the stool next to him.

'Would you like a drink?' he asks. I sense a slight embarrassment. Not his usual style. Joe is standing before them.

'A Martini,' she says.

'I'll have a bourbon,' the man says.

They sit silently watching Jo mix the martini and pour it from a height into the long stemmed wide lipped glass he places in front of her on a mat. He reaches a bottle from the shelf in front of the tall, long mirror and pours a generous shot into a heavy glass and pushes it towards the man. They both reach for their glasses and looking at each other touch them together.

Binoculars

She steps back from the canvas, lights a cigarette, tilts her head to one side and through narrowed eyes, stares at the painting on the easel.

'Shit,' she mouths shifting her gaze from the image to the mirror hanging on the wall to the left of the easel. She leans closer.

'Fucking Madonna.' She curses and jams the brush into a tin can of turps. She rubs her hands hard on the blue and white striped butcher's apron she wears.

She turns, walks to the open window, stares out over red ochre rooftops to the harbour below, and beyond that embrace, to the heat hazed shimmer of undulating ocean and dark thrust of mountains in the distance.

'Too bloody perfect.'

She raises both hands to her face, touches tentatively her fingertips to the closed eyes, runs them on lightly along the ridge of snub nose, down to the curve of mouth, traces with her forefinger the generous lips, then on to jut of determined chin, she pinches between paint-stained thumb and forefinger. Again and again, dreamlike, eyes closed she repeats the motion of exploration.

A frown creases her brow. She half turns and reaches for the binoculars he had left on the window sill. She aims them onto the outer curve of the harbour wall where his yacht is moored, fore and aft. No sign of life. The hatch to the saloon is closed, sails furled around the boom, the blue and white striped Greek flag hangs limp at the peak of the mast. She shifts the binoculars to scan the jetty. She stiffens and adjusts the focusing knob. He is walking towards the yacht, a woman at his side. He reaches down, grasps and pulls on the mooring rope, drawing the stern into the stone wall and, reaching his other hand, he guides her onto the deck, jumping after her. He glances around then bends and pulling back the hatch, motions her, with a sweep of his arm, to go down. She lifts her long white skirt and, glancing up at him, smiling, steps down. He follows and she sees, in slow motion detail, his hand reach up and slide the hatch closed.

'Shit shit shit. Fucking bitch. Blonde, cute cunt.'

She swings the binoculars down to the small round portholes. Nothing. The boat is rocking very slightly, tiny undulations in the otherwise mirror sheen. She directs the lenses up to the mast she is certain is moving in tiny, slow circles. Down again she moves her fired vision, not noticing a boat on the other side of the harbour has just pulled away, its wake setting up a flurry of wavelets around the white hull of his boat – a confusion of jostling shimmers. The mast sways, the bowsprit dips downwards then up, then down again. A gull settles on one of the cross trees, burrows its beak vigorously under a wing; sways with the motion of the boat.

She bangs the binoculars down on the sill and turns back to the canvas. She takes a brush from the can, she squeezes a thick globule of paint onto her palette. She darkens the smooth incline of skin beneath the cheek bones, puts aside the brush, takes up a palette knife and, with swift jabs, disturbs what had been sheen of black hair falling to each side of the face. With a minute sable brush she whitens individual strands. The same brush she alerts the half lowered lids of the eyes; lifts them and darkens to a sheen the pupils within the soft brown irises. At each side, she etches a fine tracery of lines. She works fast with skilled ease. The mouth's sensuousness she accentuates, parts the lips, revealing a hint of the white tips of teeth. On and on she works glancing to the image in the mirror.

'Bye bye, Madonna. Welcome Jane,' she whispers.

The mountains in the background, she blurs to a lowering dark presence of shadow and ridge.

She stands back. Lights a cigarette. Smiles.

'Yes' she mouths. 'Got it. Thank you, bastard and cunt.'

Monarch Butterfly

Pencil poised, she pressed her lips together and her knees involuntarily followed attempting to smother, unsuccessfully, a tiny puff of a fart tickling between her buttocks. She glanced around and surreptitiously dropped her pencil, bent, sniffed and disappointed straightened, smoothed her skirt and blew her nose into a dainty handkerchief kept in her sleeve.

'Hallelujah.' A voice from beyond the window cried, his face peering in. 'Hoorah, I heard it. The cry of a mating Monarch butterfly, at last I've heard it.' His unshaven cheeks were ruddy, nose wide and red and his eyes, beneath a flaxen rick of hair, dazzling blue.

With one step he entered through the open window, reached across the desk, grasped her shoulders in a grip that frightened and excited her.

'Hurrah,' he said quietly, his mouth to her ear. 'Now, Miss Molly, now the barriers are down, no holding back, you hear, no holding back.'

Lifting her from her swivel chair he swept her out of the window over his shoulder and lollopped across the lawn. Her eyes astonished, her body tinglingly compliant, she felt the motion as if she were riding a hunter through a field of tall ripe corn, and when he laid her down under the wide spread branches of a chestnut tree, she felt no fear, no fear at all as he lifted her skirt, deftly removed her panties and placed himself within her. They rode together smooth and fast, slow and careful, and when they were done, she put back on her panties and smoothed her skirt. He lifted her up, lolloped back to the window, stepped through and replaced on the chair. With a nod and a twinkle he departed into the summer air.

Hope Cove

The setting sun startled the bare branches of the trees on either side of the sinuous ribbon of lane, deepened the pools of shadow beneath the high banks. She twitched the headlights into high beams and glanced to the boy at her side, road map on his knees. From behind she could just hear the bass notes seeping from the headphones, one each, pressed to the ears of the twins snuggled under a woolly blanket in each other's arms.

'Where are we, Joe?'

His finger on the map moved about vaguely. He glanced up at her. For an instant she saw his face, the boy's father, that bully, now gone to dominate another. She heard his voice, felt momentarily the electric jolt of panic in her body. 'That's your bloody job, woman, to know where we are.' That arsehole always blaming, never even listening to her directions.

'Look, there's a signpost,' Joe, relieved, called out.

She stopped the car and peered up at the post, half obscured by overhanging branches, just outside the beam of the headlights. 'St Mary's Polk' she picked out on the left finger pointing to an even narrower lane than the one they were on. Hope Cove 3½ miles, the legend on the other.

'There, that's the way, we turn right here,' Joe commanded mildly. 'I knew where we were,' he added.

'Thanks Joe.' She ruffled his hair. 'Hope we get there soon, it'll be difficult pitching the tent if it's too dark,' she said.

'I can do it,' Joe said cheerily.

She wondered if she'd brought the mallet.

He'd have had it all organised – oh yes – down to the last bloody peg. She had kinda liked it knowing he'd have it all sorted but there was precious little joy and no bloody mystery in the endless lists and neatly packed order of the camping excursions with him and Joe and the girls. She'd always been nervous of getting anything wrong. She pictured the jumble of gear in the boot of the car. *Oh well we'll manage*, she thought, as she drove slowly between the steep banks into the enveloping darkness. *Where there is abandon, there is hope*, she thought wryly to herself wondering where the line came from. Little aphorisms, if you could call them that, often popped into her head.

The lane curved to the left and there it was; a twinkle of lights in a field and beyond the immense space of the sea, the last light luminous on the wave tips.

She turned through the gate, bumped down to a gap between a caravan and a big bell tent where a group of adults and children milled about pulling on ropes laughing and shouting as it rose and swayed and seemed about to collapse.

'Here we are,' she called out, but Joe and the girls were already out and running down to the beach.

She got out of the car, raised her eyes to the blue black sky, where a half moon glowed comfortingly and felt a surge of immense relief like a wave of light washing through her body. She knew she could do it. On her own. Care for the three, relieve them of the pressure he had put them all under, to get it right. This was it. A new beginning.

Irme

Irme and I sat at a small round table outside her old, wooden Bavarian farmhouse in late spring sunshine, a bottle of whisky between us. I had not seen her for years though we communicated regularly with intense letters. We had first met years before on the Greek island of Hydra, where I then lived and where she had a small house she visited every summer. She was then a psychiatrist working in Munich and from that first meeting she had attempted to answer, or at least discuss, the burning questions of the young troubled romantic that I was then.

We had been talking about childhood influences when, just as she'd lit a cigarette, she said through a billow of smoke.

'I'm going to tell you a story.' She often came up with tales that penetrated and embroidered whatever it was we were talking about.

'I spent years and years trying to make sense of what cannot be said or perhaps even known by the mind. I think that is why I first became a doctor and moved into psychiatry. For instance I could not understand why I was attracted to dusty working men.' She glanced towards Anselm, a cheerful, ex-submariner, her partner for many years, who was building a stone wall some distance away at the edge of the raggedy lawn bright with meadow flowers.

'I realize now that the first images a child receives engrave themselves in the psyche.' She paused and poured us both generous shots of malt whisky.

'We lived in Munich, my parents and I. They were both academics. Anti-fascist but they kept quiet. They had to. Every morning, on waking to the sound of the chimes of the tall clock on the landing I would pull back the heavy curtains, open the double doors and go out onto the narrow balcony that overlooked the ruins opposite. I had heard the planes and bombs, and the gun fire and seen the fires and seen also the corpses lying on the road. It was a terrible time. I was frightened all the time. Our building was spared but the one just across from us had not.' She paused. 'Why am I telling you this?' She touched my hand with the tip of a finger. 'I'm not sure. I just want to. I've not spoken of it before.'

She went on. 'One morning, some months after peace had been made, I stood on the balcony and noticed a workman standing close to one of the remaining walls of the ruined house opposite. I did not understand what he was doing at first then realized he was urinating. He turned, buttoning himself and looked up and saw me. For some days, four or five, I saw the man every morning. He always urinated then turned to button and look up to me. He was not there on the sixth morning and I missed him. It was a Sunday. I could hear the church bells. He appeared again on the next morning and I was glad. It was summer and I was dressed in a nightgown. White cotton, I remember. When he had finished urinating and had turned I saw he had his penis in his hand and was rubbing it, all the while looking up at me. I felt *die Kraft*, the force of his gaze. The movements of his hand became more rapid. I did not know what he was doing but I felt in my belly a strange sensation. I could not take my eyes of him.

I saw him tilt his head back, his mouth open. I saw a jet of something flying from the end of his penis. In slow motion, I saw it flying in an arc falling to the earth at his feet. I felt his eyes on me as he gave a last rub before tucking his penis away then he turned and was gone back into the ruin of the building.'

She took a drink, raising her glass to me. 'To life's mysteries.' We clinked.

'I have had many lovers. There was only one rule, which is that they share my love of Rilke's poetry. Most did even if they had never read poetry before. My dusty lovers were not the poetic types.' She laughed. 'Nearly always, before making love, we would read one of his poems. I feel deeply all his writing. *I Live My life* is a poem of his I often recite to myself. It reminds me that life is a mystery. Those lines celebrate what cannot be known but how rich they make life.' She spoke the poem, eyes closed, first in German then in English.

I live my life in growing orbits,
Which move out over the things of the world.
Perhaps I can never achieve the last
But that will be my attempt.

I am circling around God, around the ancient tower,
And I have been circling for a thousand years,
And I still don't know if I am a falcon or a storm,
Or a great song.

'I've tried to live my life like that. Living the questions. Perhaps that is why I have told you this story. No answer, just the question.' She paused.

'That time was such a...' She hesitated and looked upwards. '*Einflußreich.*' her brow crinkled. 'Nein. *Scheiße*. What is it? Ach. I want to get it right.'

'Potent.' I said.

'Ja. Ok.' She mouthed the word as if tasting it for flavour. 'Ja. That will do.' She looked at me her blue eyes intense, penetrating and not for the first time I wished the forty or so years between us could be contracted.

She smiled and again touched my hand with the tip of her index finger. 'Ja. That was a potent time of my life. My strange and unsettling conspiracy with that workman. I can recall now the immediate sense of anticipation I had awakening in the darkness. I did not connect the feelings I was having as to do with *Sexualität*, sexuality. Hah, that word crosses over easily. She laughed. 'And so it should. I'd had no feelings before like those I felt stirring then. Even now I can recall all that occurred. I used to stand very still and concentrated in a state of nervous eagerness. A mix of dread and, what was it? Another feeling, new to me, in my belly. I had a vague sense that something was not right, not wrong exactly but something my parents should not be told. That increased the excitement. Yes, it was excitement. I had never touched myself sexually and did not then although I did relate the feeling to a sensation in my lower belly. It became a ritual each morning and the one morning of the week when he did not come was almost...' She paused again. 'Excruciating. Is that the word in English?'

'Yes,' I replied.

'Interesting, it is the same word in German, exactly. A good word. It fits well. I cannot recall his face, strange isn't it? He had untidy gingerish hair and his nose was big, I remember that much. I suppose my attention was lower down.'

She laughed. 'One morning he was not there and the next morning and the one after that, no sign of him and I felt deserted, abandoned. I still had the feelings when I stood on the balcony waiting but they gradually became a black hole, a longing that could not be filled. I was surprised when one morning I felt my own hand between my legs, touching and was astonished and a little frightened at the strength of the feeling which was not like anything I had experienced before. I was balanced on a thin branch over an *Abgrund*, a chasm that was so high I felt dangerous and intoxicated at the same time. The detonation, and *mein Gott*, it was just that, when it came, was like falling off, falling and flying all at once. That first *Orgasmus*, hah, see – same word again. That orgasm transformed my life. At that moment I became a woman and I was only twelve.'

She lifted her glass. 'To that perverted man. And to the questions that have no answers.'

The Execution

As I was walking homewards from the Tower I looked back and saw the ravens, aerial sentries gliding in a descending gyre, loudly celebrating their anticipation of eyes and coils of innards.

It had been a splendid spectacle – all three of them Papists, who had, we were told by the Lord High Chamberlain, confessed to a plot to overthrow the Queen. 'Under torture, thumbscrews, rack and fire,' I heard murmured amongst the mob gathered by the river. An old fisher woman, I deduced by the reek wafting from her, told, in a delighted screech, that their screams could be heard beyond the tower walls.

The man, a tall fellow, led out first onto the scaffold, newly strewn with straw to soak up the blood that would soon flow, was dressed in a dark red ermine cloak. He held his head high though his hands, bound before him, were bloodily mangled. His wife, in a torn white gown, was weeping piteously, blood running down her legs. She had, I suppose been a fetching woman, but now her face was blotched and tears ran in bloody rivulets down her ravaged face. High born both, from the North my neighbour told me, de Mont something or other. Her guilt, once displayed to the baying mob, she was taken back within. As a woman, it being deemed inappropriate to expose her nakedness, she was spared noose and knife, and would, in the hungry embrace of the flames at the stake, meet her maker.

Their son, a mere boy of 15 or 16, came last on his knees, dragged like a whipped cur by the gaoler. He wailed over and over in a shrill voice. 'I'm innocent. Innocent.'

The crowd, momentarily hushed by the sight of the broken lad, began booing and the fisherwoman bawled out. 'Do for him and make it slow.' Heartless crone.

It was a muggy afternoon. Black bulging bladders of clouds hung portentously. The tide was low and a host of gulls screamed and squabbled on the stinking mud.

The boy – last out first in – the noose about his neck, was hauled up to dangle, his feet kicking, a few inches above the boards. The executioner, Dan Drury it was, much loved by the rabble for his showmanship and adroit skill with the disembowelling knife, had the lad split from neck to crutch in a trice, coils of innards spilling out. With one deft slice, Drury severed the boy's genitals holding them up above his head to a roar of approval. What a sight it was, and the boy's cries, I swear, reached way beyond the range of the human voice. I saw a giggle of children, playing a game of peek-a-boo, covering their eyes and ears then uncovering them, screaming delightedly.

I wonder sometimes about human desires. Sex I understand, mostly; that compulsion that leads one again and again to seek out the erotic mystery of the woman, which is not to say that it necessarily requires that complicity with one's wife. I have had many most satisfactory humpings with whores. But this spectacle; witnessing of the extremes of human suffering, is edifying. All the senses provoked to such extremes I feel a sense of giddy elation. The smells, the expectant rapt expressions on the faces of the mob and their cries and hoots, here by the river flowing in and flowing out. The sounds; the groans of the man, the screams of the boy mingling with the sky high caws of the ravens, combine to encapsulate the extremes of human experience.

The father was next. He had held out his bloody hands to his wife when she was dragged away to the stake. The expression on his face was piteous. What could be worse than this, I wondered, knowing with grim satisfaction that we were yet to witness such humiliation and agony that would fill us all with dread and exultation that it was not one of us about to be so dexterously dismembered.

We were not disappointed. With cool precision Mr Drury brought the man, like his son before him, to within a whisper of suffocation; the knotted rope tight about his neck, his eyes starting from his head, as he was sliced and adroitly divided – like one would a roasted chicken, the limbs from the torso. As they were both drawn higher on the gibbet it amazed me how they still hung onto life. The boy was past screaming, his face was all rounds, eyes, mouth, as if he had reached some pinnacle of pain that no sound could possibly give cry to, though I wondered if there was yet sufficient air in his body to give vent. There they hung dangling, slowly strangling, swinging in the fetid breeze from the river.

I had a fierce appetite and decided to stop at my favourite pie shop. When I next glanced back again at the scene, the ravens had descended and were at their squabbling business pecking vigorously at the corpses; so I presumed

41

them now to be. One atop each head, two cowl black birds stabbed at the eyes and others on the shoulders bobbing and crying as they dipped their heads into the bloody cavities.

Accompanied by a jug of rich ruby claret, I wondered, as I savoured the succulent beef pie, which of the entertainments on offer in the city I most enjoyed: theatre or execution? I could not decide. There would be no public killings for a while so it would next have to be the theatre. There was a new play at the Globe, I'd heard, by the up-and-coming penman, William something. Macbeth, I had heard, by title. A bloodthirsty yarn by all accounts. That was something to look forward to.

I decided I would to the Globe next day, via the tower, to see how much remained of them.

Pashupatinath, Nepal 1973

First Visit

Bruise blue the agitation within, grave dark the twist in the belly, but – that most transformative of words – by the time I reached the temple by the river, via the stalls on the dusty road, where I bought a puffed poori and a single cigarette, the sun in the bowl of the sky was a golden sphere, the carrion crows, angels of clemency, and the monkeys, watching from branches and clinging to the gilded triumph of spires joining heaven to earth, emissaries of the gods...

I sat with Saddhus, some naked as at birth, ash-blotched, others in saffron, rocking within the smoke road by the river flowing through.

A mother in a white sari, fanning her son, eight or nine, still breathing, though it was not long before he was laid on the neatly piled wood of his pyre she circled three times, sprinkling oil, blessing him and flames...

I sat there and watched knowing nothing. When the flames had sated their hunger, she took the ashes and sprinkled them onto the river.

Listen

Listen, the air is vivid with their chatter
as they weave through shadows, dart
from jasmine to hibiscus to frangipani,
to tender fronds of young palm.

Their tunes and various temples
threading the heavens to the sky.

Along the lane by the garden, an old woman,
wrapped in the intricate folds of her sari,
with one hand balances a precarious pile
of kindling on her head, and with the other
she taps a bamboo cane on the buttocks
of an ox ambling before her, horns crimson tipped.
Bangles of silver and bright plastic jingle on her thin wrists.

I am between two worlds – the one I have come from
and carry within – dying, gangrenous –
and this one of braided streams.

Listen – the whisper of a plane way up there seeping a scar.

The gardener, hunkered on the paved path,
his toes like fingers splayed, sweeps
with a few sticks bound together – swish swish –
in an arc around his compact body.
Leaves fall in arabesques, clatter onto the dry earth.
No end to this task. Swish swish – new leaves
bud, unfurl, green, crisp, tumble.

Hampi, Karnataka

'No poem, he said, but in things.' – *William Carlos Williams*

I sit wearing a jade green lunghi. Yellow chair. Black tiles.
Before me, down a rock-strewn slope,
tail-flicking buffalo stand and stare at the unhurried river
that coils dreamily – basking, twisting, sinuous as crocodile –
stirred of a sudden round tumble of rocks to roar and jeer
at such opposition to the millions of meandering years.
On the far side, wide tiers of steps climb to temple pillars –
an order of angled shadows dense as blind vision
where sensually, sinuously, dance celebrants
of love and death – Siva, Kali, Krishna, Parvati.
A chaotic mountain of boulders rears above,
disgorged long before gods dreamt.

Far as eye reach, a silent incision of jet trail.

On a platform of smooth rock jutting into the river,
women in saris – orange, yellow, purple and green –
squat to beat clothes clean – the sound
of the thwacks reaching me, as sound does,
later than the colours of which this vision is made.

Completed

They found each other at the re-hab.
Alex, sliced slim, finger picking nervous,
her twenty-seven-year-old body a judder of jangled nerves.
And Emma solid, almost square.
(They would have fitted well on a tandem bicycle.)
They got each other. It was obvious. All could see.
They laughed at their predicament
on the precipice of their recovery –
Twelve steps forward ten back and so on.
A life-long sentence – 'in recovery',
those that make it – day to vertiginous day.
Hardly any fissures for finger tips to find purchase.
They had each other until they crossed a line,
the ever watchful carers deemed dangerous
and separated them. They know best, that
lovers lose their wills. Two on a tightrope might trip.
Alex tumbled into the void of her helpless, love-less isolation.
She fled the safety, no longer a sanctuary. She fled back
to the streets. the dealers, the fix. The disappearance.
She disappeared.
Heart failure the certificate starkly stated. Yes, heart failure.

Indian Eye

If, for one blink,
I saw as you see
in your cobalt eyes,
I would die in that apparition.
The idea of self would shatter.

You observe so closely, so remotely.
Is it 'I' that those lenses receive,
or some other arrangement of creation?
Your unblinking eyes gaze into me,
revealing an abyss.

Never so close as this where I come from –
the managed world.
Your dark discretion always at a distance –
            branch or wire –
or commanding your faultless composition
            from way up there.

Here, in this random
clashed land of spiced hearts,
you reign, pecking on rotting corpses
or, as now, a few inches
from my plate of rice, unruffled.

Kra! Kra!
You called your name,
long before human utterance.
I fade to a shade in the swoop
of your flight. And a grain of rice.

The Air So Sweet

The air so sweet, the sky a blue blush.
Birds, when I pause to listen,
fill the emptiness with song.
My gloom is greedy for nature's good news.

I like to keep informed and today,
I've heard by 8 am of murder, rape,
torture, and, on my rural doorstep, corruption
in the care given to the young by a priest.

I pause, reach a hand to touch
a leaf unfurling from its tight coil, one
of countless clues that keep secret
nature's order in the chaos.

The path is steep and narrow
skidding down to a sliver of a stream.
Faithful to my balance, I cross
foot after foot on a thigh-thick trunk.

But still, I tell myself, noticing above,
the wing-wide hover of a buzzard –
there is love. We can be true to another
even as we hide how deep our daily fear.

Returning to my desk and lighted screen
I believe, for a while at least, the dream
I have revived, of our skill, again
and again to foster the beautiful and the new.

Prayer

I thought it was a crumple of coat lying in the road
as I walked down the long sinew of hill from home.
As I got close, eyes turned back from circling hawk,
I saw it was a badger on his back.
I knelt, touched the soft spikes of fur.
His eyes looked blindly into mine.
I thought of the distances he'd travelled –
so much safer beneath the earth
than on this thread of lane.
Taking his paws, I lifted and laid him
in the dew-bright grass of the verge.
Pressed a hand upon him,
Searching for the beat of his heart.

Slow the road home,
the soft throbbing of a broken dawn.

Bundled

Bundled to meet the wind and the rain,
energies much greater than my anger
at this season's betrayal.
Hunched to the brink of the valley,
filled with mist, I trudge.
I stare into the invisibility from where
a flight of gulls, bright as sparks,
on their god-guided wings, soar.

Itch

The itch began soon after, grew
more urgent. Compelled fingers to burrow.

Imagine my surprise, pinched before my eyes,
a minuscule microcosm of life.

Closer closer till I saw the pincers
and the shape that was a crab.

Not one but a tribe had leapt
from her jungle to mine as we collided
in this swamp of passionate life.

I Wish

I wish I might go mad to praise
steep in a wooden tub of sea-wind
with bats in my hair
the sound of whales mating
in my left ear
and in the right
the scuffling of a mole
under the executioner's
perfect lawn

Father

Did we collect chestnuts together?
Why do I even imagine we might have?
The image grows –
Tying them with string into holes pierced
Through tough skin to white flesh and out again.

He was a tree I wanted so much to climb –
Not chestnut or oak – more likely a conifer,
One with branches close to the trunk,
Juniper or Cyprus,
Reaching tall, spreading narrowly.

I shrink to think of us playing that game.
Face to face, conkers dangling.
What if I had broken his?
I have no idea.
Such a familiar stranger he was – Daddy.

We skirted about one another, he and I –
And when we met – eye to eye,
Recognising noses and shaggy brows –
And maybe, a look of sadness and of
Bewilderment deep in our eyes.

I wish we had found some game to play,
Not chess, nor tennis or golf or scrabble –
One with dice and all the chance
Fate plays. We might have discovered
How much we are of each other.

Falling

There are those whose lives are threaded to turmoil
by fate or imbalance of axis, which feels to them
as an unnatural distortion of shape like flare of fire
that knits a recurring twist of complaint.
A provocation of random images
Cajoled in the mind to a mêlée, to no order.

They might hear rain on the roof as orders
or birds tweeting questions that must, in the turmoil,
be answered and obeyed to stay the arrival of images
that inflict such pain that they compel them
to take up a blade, to silence the complaint;
and if that incision of flesh fails they reach to the fire.

Whether it be by knife or lick of fire
gush of blood or bubble of skin to restore order
there might be brief respite from perpetual complaint.
Life for all is a trap of the good-versus-evil turmoil
for even in peace despair lurks, awaiting them,
beguiled as they are by the imagined beauty of images

that, by distortion of perception leads within images
to the dancing contortions of fire.
A truth there, in leap or slow embers, for them
who have, in the chaos, found an order –
a craft (maybe with oars) to smile at ocean turmoil,
to feel body's ease, to release complaint.

Without romance, guile or restraint
to glance into the pool, enter the images –
reflections of moon and stars free of turmoil
and even, mind quiet, to gaze into the fire,
anticipating neither grief nor peace; to encounter order.
All have been there. It waits, even for the un-quiet them,

those who live in the hell of fail. For them,
who may yet find peace, beyond complaint,
where the compass is still and an order
settles within the contortion of images
when there is no more gruel for the fire
nor notion of heaven or hell to fuel turmoil.

I question the turmoil of fire, the complaints
of those who have failed and even the dis-order.
Those images. The world falling in on itself.

Alex

Silently slowly darkly
Addiction slipped through the back door

I never did nothing wrong
But it still ate her to her core

Only the sound of the waves
Of life slowly draining away

Was it the first word I heard
On that dark deathly day.

Rick Vick

Dedication

Also in memory of Rick's daughter, Faye Jean Vick, 13th April 1989–27th October 2020. Faye's creativity embodied many artistic forms, and with respect to her father's influence, chief amongst those was her love and practice of the written word.

Poem for Rick

Faye Vick

Black Crows in the morning
Black crows at night
You in your leather jacket
Bliss you called your brandy
and cigar & I know you
as father, rebel, and most
profoundly as believer in the
underdog, how well you taught
us about the struggle
& the plight of humanity
because you felt it in your
bones, you felt it for the
underdog and that is
humble that is love and
you taught me that, and
now I am with you a
black crow on my
shoulder and it is you
because I know you &
because of love.

And now I pick up where
you left off in so many
ways, your daughter and
because I know you
I will do what you taught me
and struggle with the struggling,
rejoice with the happy
and love and
above all else make art
as you dear father taught
me. My Rick.

THE NELSON TRUST

Rick was a Creative Writing tutor at The Nelson Trust for many years, helping people in residential treatment to find their voice by putting pen to paper.

Our current CEO, John Trolan, began his involvement with the Nelson Trust as a volunteer facilitating creative writing workshops. He says:

I know the enabling power of creative writing, the opportunity it offers to clients to find their voice, to express who they are, where they've been and where they'd like to go and perhaps most importantly to be listened to and heard, sometimes for the first time in their lives. Rick facilitated this beautifully. It's why he was with us for so long. We miss him.

We are very grateful to honour Rick's legacy by using this gift to help people in their recovery from addiction.

The Nelson Trust brings belief, hope and long-term recovery to lives affected by substance misuse, abuse, deprivation, violence, and poverty. Our residential rehabilitation programme has helped individuals to tackle the root causes of their substance misuse since 1985. In 2010, we began to deliver Women's Community Services to women facing multiple disadvantages. We now have three Women's Centres; in Gloucester, Swindon and Bridgwater and are establishing a fourth centre in Bristol.

Lightning Source UK Ltd.
Milton Keynes UK
UKHW032100080221
378442UK00004B/114